Ndovu the Elephant-An African Tale

By

Philip L. Levin

May your dreams take you to the far corners of the world!

Philip L. Levin 2011

Ndovu the Elephant-An African Tale

By Philip L. Levin

Published by
Doctor's Dreams Publishing
710West Beach Blvd.
Long Beach, MS 39560
228-596-7217
www.DoctorsDreams.net

Technical Production Bruce Keyes

Manufactured in South Korea in March 2011 by Pacom

IBSN 978-0-9834396-0-8

First Edition

Ndovu the Elephant-An African Tale

Exploring the Serengeti
Photos and Text: Philip L. Levin

Ndovu was born on the Serengeti of Africa, a land of plentiful grass. His mother, Kikumba, taught him the ways of the world.

"The Wildebeests are gentle like us," she said. "They eat grass and will never hurt you."

"Not all animals are gentle.
You must beware Hatari the lion."

"Will Hatari try to eat me?" Ndovu asked. "Not as long as you stay with the herd," his mother said. "Together we are strong."

Ndovu didn't want to stay with the herd.
He wanted adventure!

Kikumba was talking with her sister. She didn't notice Ndovu wander away.

Ndovu found the baboons and zebras playing. He wanted to play too! He called out, but the baboons climbed the trees and the zebras galloped away.

He followed the zebras to their watering hole. Ndovu rushed in, splashing and playing in the mud.

He came upon Kiboko Hippopotamus with her family. "Where are you going, little elephant?" she asked. "I am flowing with the water," Ndovu announced.

Ndovu followed the river to the Great Lake Nakuru, where the pink flamingos gathered by the thousands. He filled his trunk with water and sprayed the birds. They squawked and flapped noisily into the air.

Nkombe, the great white rhinoceros, came down to the lake to drink.

Ndovu and Nkombe played together all afternoon, eating grass and rolling in the mud.

A herd of gazelles came by, curious to see an elephant and a rhinoceros frolicking together.

Bweha kept guard, his ears alert for danger.

Najano, the yellow billed stork, watched them play.

Mbuni Ostrich came up to Ndovu and asked,
"Where is your family, little elephant?"

Ndovu missed his family.
He decided to search for them.

He asked Kenge, the lizard,
"Have you seen my family?"
Kenge just flicked his round tail
and scurried away.

Ndovu came upon
Twiga the giraffe,
munching on the leaves
of the highest trees.
"Hello up there,"
Ndovu called. "Can you
see my family?"

"No Ndovu. I hope you find them soon.
The Serengeti can be dangerous at night."

The sun began setting.
Ndovu wanted his mother

He asked Ndege, "Have you seen my mother?"
The Secretary Bird merely shook her quills
and scampered away.

When he asked Kima,
the blackfaced monkey,
she spit at him.

"Can you help me find my family?" he asked Mbogo, the gnu.

"Yesterday I saw a herd of elephants over the next hill," he said.

Over the hill all he found was a group of vultures.
"I've lost my family," Ndovu said.
"You best be careful," the biggest vulture said. "The big cats will be out hunting their dinner soon."

The lioness was waking
with growling belly.

The cheetahs sniffed the air.

Ndovu rushed to hide
in some nearby bushes,
but Nyati the water buffalo
was already there.

Ndovu looked up to find Tai, the vulture, watching him.
The baby elephant trumpeted in fright.

Kikumba heard his calls and answered.
Ndovu shouted with joy,
and raced across the tundra to join his herd.

"You are too young to roam the Serengeti by yourself," his mother said. Ndovu nuzzeled against her, glad to be safe.

The End

About the Author: Philip L. Levin serves as the president of the Gulf Coast Writers Association in southern Mississippi. These photos were taken during a visit he made to Kenya where he volunteered his physician services in a small rural hospital.